INKY'S GREAT ESCAPE

THE Incredible (AND MOSTLY TRUE) Story OF AN Octopus Escape

by CASEY LYALL   illustrated by SEBASTIÀ SERRA

STERLING CHILDREN'S BOOKS
New York

Inky was the greatest escape octopus of all time.

He'd slithered his way out of every trap ever invented and lived to tell the tale.

And he really liked telling the tales.

One day after wrestling with a particularly tricky trap, Inky decided it was time for a break. His arms needed a rest, so he retired to the local aquarium.

Every day, he and his tank-mate, Blotchy, would play hide-and-seek followed by a rousing game of charades.

Every night, they played Crazy Eights, and Inky would tell Blotchy all about his daring escapes.

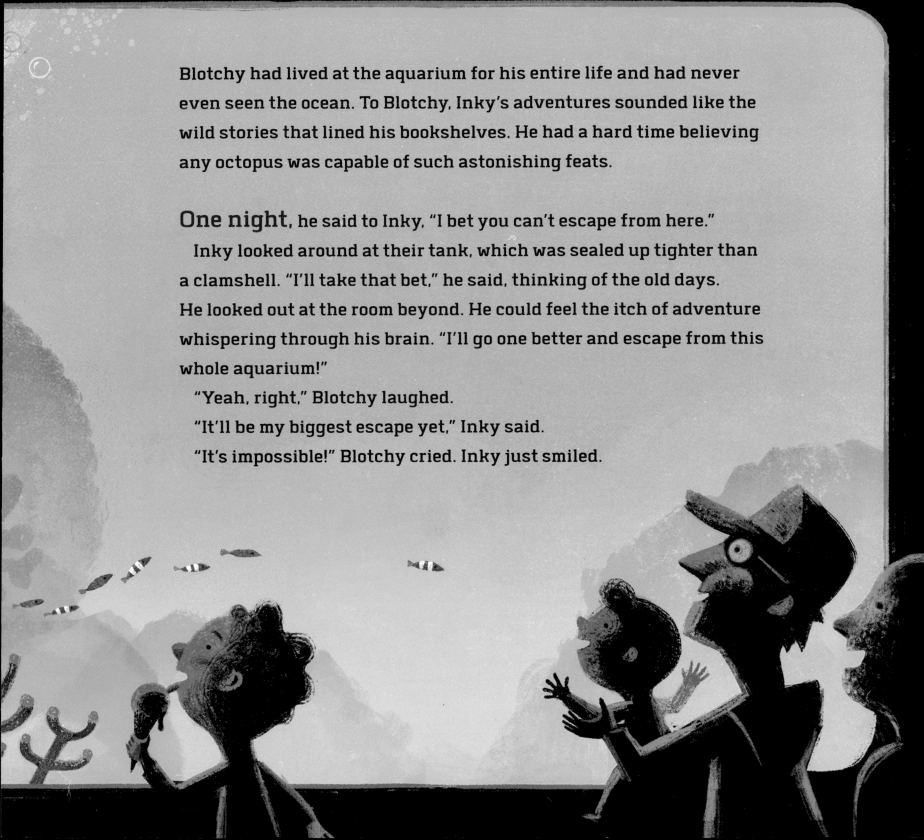

Blotchy had lived at the aquarium for his entire life and had never even seen the ocean. To Blotchy, Inky's adventures sounded like the wild stories that lined his bookshelves. He had a hard time believing any octopus was capable of such astonishing feats.

One night, he said to Inky, "I bet you can't escape from here."
Inky looked around at their tank, which was sealed up tighter than a clamshell. "I'll take that bet," he said, thinking of the old days. He looked out at the room beyond. He could feel the itch of adventure whispering through his brain. "I'll go one better and escape from this whole aquarium!"
"Yeah, right," Blotchy laughed.
"It'll be my biggest escape yet," Inky said.
"It's impossible!" Blotchy cried. Inky just smiled.

What Blotchy didn't realize was that impossible escapes were Inky's favorite kind. After many years of practice, Inky had discovered the two keys to an amazing octopus escape: patience and opportunity.

So Inky waited. He drew up his plan and called it "Inky's Incredible Idea for an Ingenious Escape."

Blotchy said the name was a bit long, but Inky knew it was just right.

Days went by, and Blotchy started to get smug. "I knew you couldn't do it," he said.

"Patience," Inky said.

"Did I ever tell you about the time I waited twelve days to escape from the lair of a giant squid?" Inky asked.

"Yes," said Blotchy. "Every week."

Inky told him again anyway.

Later that evening, the opportunity Inky had been waiting for arrived. One of the keepers left the lid to their tank open a crack. It was just a *tiny* crack, but that was enough for Inky to work with.

"The time has come," Inky said to Blotchy. "I'm about to make cephalopod history!"

He swam over to the side of the tank and began to climb . . . well, the only way an octopus can climb: one sucker after another. Inch by inch, he pulled himself up to the top.

With magnificent skill that only the most remarkable octopuses possess, he poked one arm through the lid and began to wedge his body out through the gap. Inky went as flat as a piece of seaweed as he prodded and elbowed his way to the other side.

After a great, slurpy pop, Inky squeezed free and clung to the outside of the tank. "Blotchy," he called out, "there's a whole world out there. Do you want to come with me? It'll be an adventure to remember!"

"No, thanks," said Blotchy. "Tomorrow's Fondue Friday. I don't want to miss it."

"Fair enough," Inky said. He slid down the side of the tank,
leaving a triumphant trail of octopus ooze in his wake.

Blotchy peered through the glass and watched as his brave friend made his way across the aquarium floor.

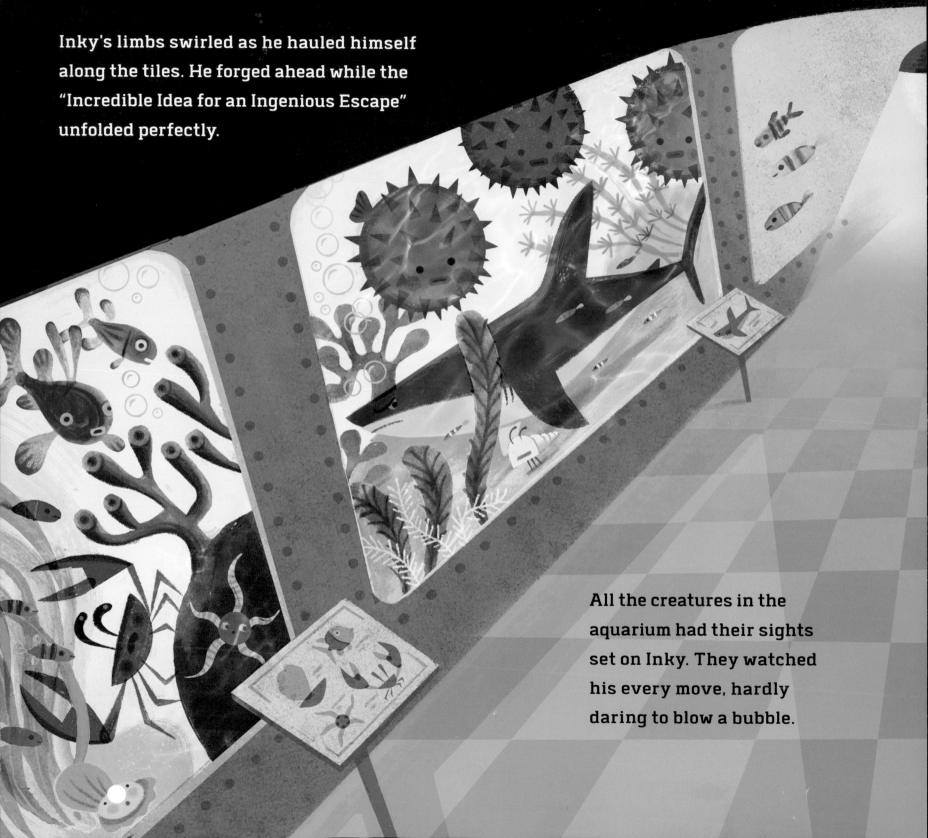

Inky's limbs swirled as he hauled himself along the tiles. He forged ahead while the "Incredible Idea for an Ingenious Escape" unfolded perfectly.

All the creatures in the aquarium had their sights set on Inky. They watched his every move, hardly daring to blow a bubble.

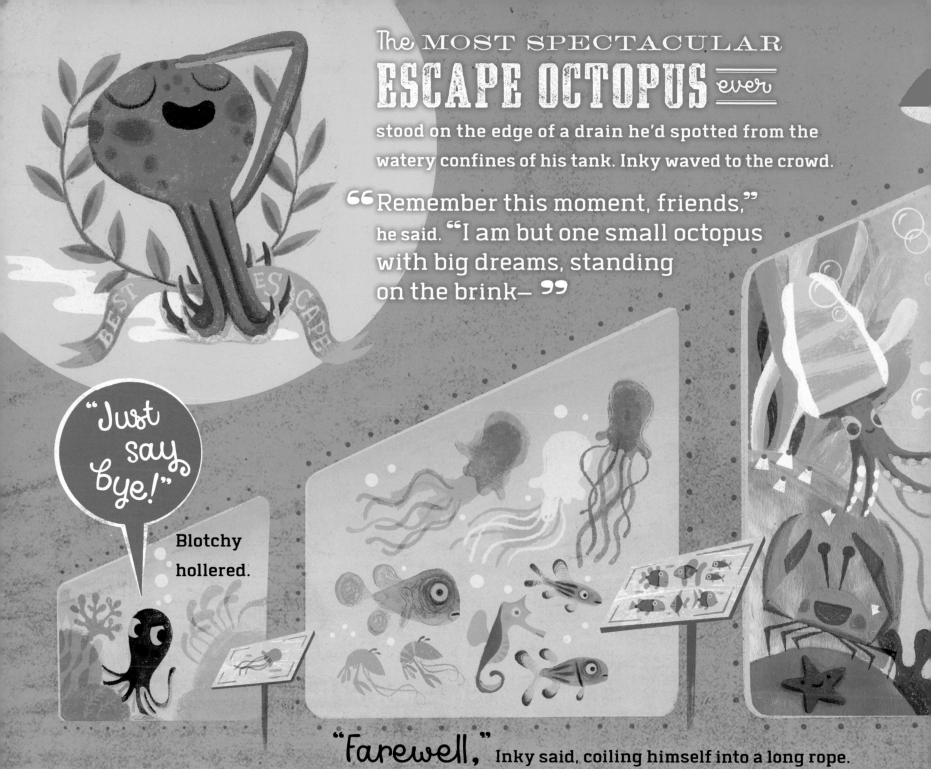

The MOST SPECTACULAR ESCAPE OCTOPUS ever

stood on the edge of a drain he'd spotted from the watery confines of his tank. Inky waved to the crowd.

"Remember this moment, friends," he said. "I am but one small octopus with big dreams, standing on the brink— "

"Just say bye!"

Blotchy hollered.

"Farewell," Inky said, coiling himself into a long rope.

Cheers rang out from every tank as he slipped down the drain and out into the ocean.

For years afterward, Blotchy told each new arrival about the amazing Inky and his great escape from the aquarium. Someone had to stick around to tell the tale, after all.

And, oddly enough, every once in a while, a little, dribbly trail would appear, leading from the drain all the way to the octopus tank. If you listened very closely, over the shuffling of cards, you'd hear a voice say,

"Did I ever tell you about the time I tangled with a lobster trap?"